Will

Battle on the Beach

Dave DeVisser

Illustrations by Cary VanderVeen

To Lucas
Exceed Expectations!

Dave DeVisser

School Forest Publishing, LLC
Schoolcraft, Michigan

Book design by Sagaponack Books & Design

ISBNs:
978-0-9996862-0-1 (soft-cover)
978-0-9996862-1-8 (hardcover)
978-0-9996862-2-5 (e-book)

Library of Congress Catalog Card Number: 2018900443

Summary: Willy, a WW2 jeep, and Sherman, a tank, are bullied and teased because of their poor wartime skills. On D-Day, their brave and selfless care of others turns them into heroes.

JUV016080 Juvenile Fiction / Historical / Military & Wars
JUV001010 Juvenile Fiction / Action & Adventure / Survival Stories
JUV039220 Juvenile Fiction / Social Themes / Values & Virtues
JUV039060 Juvenile Fiction / Social Themes / Friendship
JUV039230 Juvenile Fiction / Social Themes / Bullying
JUV016150 Juvenile Fiction / Historical / United States / 20th Century

www.davedevisser.com

First Edition
Printed in the USA

This book is dedicated to my father, Henry DeVisser, who served in the army from 1941 through 1945, in the South Pacific.

Henry DeVisser, 1918–2012

CONTENTS

Introduction 1

Chapter 1 ~ Willy's New Life 5

Chapter 2 ~ Sherman's New Life 9

Chapter 3 ~ Friendship 13

Chapter 4 ~ A Close Call 17

Chapter 5 ~ Promises 21

Chapter 6 ~ Sherman's Struggle 25

Chapter 7 ~ Willy's Struggle 29

Chapter 8 ~ Crossing the Channel 33

Chapter 9 ~ The Landing 39

Chapter 10 ~ Battle on the Beach 43

Chapter 11 ~ Sherman's Charge 47

Chapter 12 ~ Saving Sherman 51

Chapter 13 ~ Brave Willy 55

Chapter 14 ~ Waiting for the End 59

Chapter 15 ~ Faithful Friends 63

Chapter 16 ~ The Big Surprise 65

Chapter 17 ~ Victory Parade 69

Interesting Facts 77

D-Day Invasion Map 81

World War 2 Photographs 82

About the Author 94

About the Illustrator 95

INTRODUCTION

*This nation will remain the land of the free only
so long as it is the home of the brave.*

—Elmer Davis

Can you imagine what your life would be like if
you were living in 1944? You would not be playing
video games, texting on a cell phone, watching
television, or logging on to a computer. Why?
Because these things haven't been invented yet!

Instead, you gather around the radio every night
with your family and listen to programs like *The
Lone Ranger*, *Dick Tracy*, and *Little Orphan Annie*.
You also listen closely to news reports from a war
the United States and other nations are fighting in
Europe. Germany and Italy want to expand their

territories and take over all the European countries. The United States and its Allies are fighting to stop them. This war involves other countries as well. It's known as World War II, also called WW2.

Thousands of young men are signing up to fight as soldiers, sailors, and airmen. Your dad, older brother, or cousin may be one of them.

The United States is building new military equipment to aid the soldiers in combat. The Willys Jeep and the Sherman tank are two important machines that will help the United States Army win the war.

Come join Willy the jeep and Sherman the tank, best friends who fought in a battle on Omaha Beach in France, on June 6, 1944. This battle began the liberation of Europe from the German dictator, Adolf Hitler. The battle was called D-Day.

Sherman raised his cannon, and with a broad smile, he turned to see a familiar face come roaring up to his side.

Chapter 1
WILLY'S NEW LIFE

*No man will make a great leader who wants to
do it all himself or get all the credit for doing it.*
—Andrew Carnegie

On a hot July day in 1943, Willy the Jeep
came to life at a factory in Toledo, Ohio.
As he rolled along the assembly line, his
pride swelled. Workers bolted new parts on or welded
them together, equipping him to transport men and
supplies for the United States Army.

"I'll be light, fast, and with my four-wheel drive,
I'll go many places other vehicles can't go. Nothing
will stop me," he said.

After the USA star was painted on his olive-green hood and the ax and shovel were strapped tight to his side, Willy's excitement revved up.

Bumping other jeeps and tipping over work carts,
he raced out of the factory.

Bumping other jeeps and tipping over work carts, he raced out of the factory.

"My name is Willy, and I'm ready for action, sir," he announced to the driver. "When do I start?"

The driver laughed and said, "Mr. Willy, you don't have to call me sir. I just work here. And you'll have to wait in line before you can win this war."

To Willy's surprise, he was parked in a large holding area with hundreds of other jeeps waiting for their job assignments. While sitting around impatiently, Willy spent his days telling other jeeps how he was going to win the war.

"I'll show you guys how to do things the right way," he boasted. "Follow me and you'll learn how to carry more supplies and get things done faster."

One by one, the other jeeps grew tired of his constant bragging. Soon the only one listening to Willy was Willy himself.

Chapter 2
SHERMAN'S NEW LIFE

No one can make you feel inferior without your consent.

—Eleanor Roosevelt

In September of 1943, Sherman the tank was built in a factory near Detroit, Michigan. His thick armor and powerful cannon made him much larger and heavier than Willy. While it had taken only two hours to assemble Willy, it took two days to build Sherman.

Unlike Willy, Sherman moved slowly and carefully, wanting to be sure where he was going and how he would get there.

"I'll have plenty of firepower with my large cannon," he said, surveying himself. "I will also be able to protect the soldiers inside me with this two-inch-thick armor. I'm proud to be a tank in this army, but I hope the war ends soon. I'm not certain I can do as well as the rest."

Sherman also found himself parked in a large holding area next to the factory, with other tanks who spent their days talking about where they would be assigned and what they would do.

"Have you heard of the fearless tank commander, George Patton?" a tank named Bulldog asked the others. "He's supposed to be the best general in the army, and only the best tanks are selected to fight with him. That's who I am going to serve with. What do you say, guys, are you with me?"

"Yeah, Bulldog, we're with you," the other tanks echoed in unison, fearing to disagree.

Sherman listened in silence.

"What about you, Sherman?" Bulldog asked, facing him. "You've been awfully quiet. You're not afraid of the war, are you?"

"I'll gladly serve my country and obey what I'm commanded to do, but war is serious business,"

Sherman said. "I hope it ends soon and peace is restored. Then we won't have to fight."

Bulldog's cannon raised and, with a loud voice, he said, "I think they should have painted you chicken yellow, instead of green like the rest of us." Then he turned to the other tanks and said, "I suggest you guys avoid anyone who is yellow."

They nodded in agreement.

No one talked to Sherman or paid any attention to him the rest of their time waiting. Feelings of loneliness and rejection were Sherman's only companions as he waited through the long days for his assignment.

* * *

Time passed slowly for Willy and Sherman. Finally, the day came; they were loaded onto a train and transported to New York City. Their service in the United States Army was soon to begin.

Chapter 3
FRIENDSHIP

The only way to have a friend is to be one.
—Ralph Waldo Emerson

New York Harbor bustled with activity: dockworkers loaded cargo ships with military equipment and supplies, ready for shipment overseas. The shrill whistles of tugboats and bellowing ships' horns filled the air. A large yellow crane slowly lowered Willy into a ship's hold, where the cargo is stored. In midair, Willy's wheels spun with anticipation, and screeched when their rubber touched the floor.

"Finally, I'm on my way to serve this country!" he shouted.

His excitement grew even more when a seaman
parked him next to a tank.

His excitement grew even more when a seaman parked him next to a tank. Looking up at the big fellow with heavy armor and a large cannon, Willy spoke boldly: "Hello, my name is Willy and I'm from Toledo, Ohio. What's your name?"

Slowly lowering his eyes to view the little green jeep, Sherman softly replied, "My name is Sherman and I'm from Detroit, Michigan."

"Well, well, we're both from the Midwest. Where do you think we're headed? I hear we're going to England. I'm so excited, I can't wait to see action and win this war," Willy chattered.

Sherman hesitated, and then replied, "We're part of a large group of ships they call a convoy. I hope we get there safely. It's a long and dangerous voyage over the ocean."

The tone in his voice gave Willy the feeling that Sherman was uneasy about things to come.

Willy looked at Sherman and, with self-assurance, said, "Don't worry about a thing. When we arrive there, I'll get my orders and show you what to do and how to do it."

Then Willy launched into the familiar story of how he would win the war and be honored by a general, maybe even the army's top general, Dwight Eisenhower!

Sherman listened quietly to Willy. Though he grew tired of the little jeep's constant bragging, there was something about Willy's confidence that Sherman liked.

So their friendship grew in the hold of the ship as they made their way across the Atlantic Ocean— destination, England.

Chapter 4
A CLOSE CALL

F-E-A-R has two meanings: "Forget Everything And Run" or "Face Everything And Rise." The choice is yours.

—Zig Ziglar

The ocean was quiet and a dense fog blanketed the water. A long line of supply ships reflected off the calm surface like a mirror as they sailed eastward. For the first three days of a scheduled ten-day voyage, there was no activity on board except for the routine duties of sailors and the constant drone of the ships' engines.

Sherman's worries about the trip began to recede, and he often dozed for long periods. Willy, on the other hand, carried on a conversation with himself as to what part he would play in the war. Outwardly, Willy appeared confident and capable of anything, but deep inside he was glad to have his big friend Sherman by his side.

Time passed slowly in the dark belly of the ship, but on the fourth day, alarms suddenly sounded and sailors rushed about securing the cargo.

"Go up on deck and uncover the lifeboats in case we're torpedoed! This ship's hold is the last place I want to be if we're hit," Willy heard one sailor say to another.

"Yeah, if this ship gets hit, it will sink like a rock," the other sailor replied.

The words had no sooner left his mouth, when they heard a dull thud and felt the ship shudder.

A hatch to the deck sprang open, and a sailor shouted down, "They just torpedoed the ship in front of us!"

Now wide awake, Sherman glanced down at Willy, who was shaking with fear.

"Stay calm, Willy," Sherman said. "There's nothing we can do."

A sailor abruptly paused from his work and stood motionless. "Quiet, everyone! Do you hear something?" he asked.

Everyone immediately ceased their activity and listened intently. The faint hum of an electric motor ... and the swishing of a propeller ... gradually becoming louder ... could be only one thing.

"It's a torpedo approaching! Let's get outta here!"

Just when they expected the torpedo to hit, the sound passed by the ship's hull and began to fade.

Tools clattered onto the floor, and men scurried up ladders and out escape hatches. Willy and Sherman closed their eyes and braced themselves for the explosion. The humming and swishing increased until it echoed throughout the ship's hold … and just when they expected the torpedo to hit, the sound slipped past the ship's hull and began to fade. Before long, they could hear the explosions from depth charges the American ships were dropping into the water to sink the German submarines.

"That was a near miss," Sherman said with a sigh of relief. He looked down at his little friend. "Are you okay?"

"Of course I am," Willy replied with a quivering voice.

Sherman nodded and said nothing.

The remaining days of the voyage were quiet and the ocean remained calm. However, when Willy and Sherman learned that three ships in the convoy had sunk, their nerves were on edge until they arrived in England.

When their ship pulled in to Portsmouth Harbour for unloading, everyone was glad the trip was over. The reality of war had touched Willy and Sherman even before they left the ship.

Chapter 5

PROMISES

When it hurts to look back and you're afraid to look ahead, you can look beside you and your best friend will be there.

—Unknown

The fishy smell of salt water and oil flooded into the ship's hold as the cargo doors opened. First, a groaning crane slowly hoisted Sherman from the dark belly of the ship, into the gray daylight. Next, Willy emerged to see a city draped in cold, damp fog, busily arming itself for wartime protection.

"It's been great traveling with you, Sherman," Willy shouted over the commotion of the busy port. "Maybe we'll be together in a victory parade someday," he said with a wink.

As Willy disappeared in the flurry of activities, Sherman smiled and yelled, "You'll carry Eisenhower, and I'll carry Patton."

The next day Sherman arrived at his assigned training base. While waiting in line to be registered, he heard a familiar voice behind him.

Sherman raised his cannon, and with a broad smile, he turned to see a familiar face come roaring up to his side.

"To the back of the line, yellow," Bulldog yelled to Sherman.

Sherman pretended not to hear, but Bulldog bolted forward and pushed Sherman from his place.

"I told you, get to the back of the line!"

Sherman, not wanting a confrontation, quietly moved to the rear. A minute later another familiar voice could be heard.

"Well, well, a fellow fighting machine from the Midwest. You wouldn't be from Detroit, would you?"

Sherman raised his cannon and, with a broad smile, he turned to see a familiar face come roaring up to his side.

"Looks like we're going to train together," Willy said, his engine humming like a happy cat.

"Boy, am I glad to see you," Sherman said. "I was worried I wouldn't have any friends here."

"Don't worry about a thing," Willy replied. "We'll stick together, and I'll take care of you."

Sherman paused, and then said, "Okay, I'll take care of you too, little buddy."

Chapter 6
SHERMAN'S STRUGGLE

For every obstacle there is a solution. Persistence is the key. The greatest mistake is giving up!
—General Dwight D. Eisenhower

Willy and Sherman trained hard every day, from sunrise to sunset. Sherman practiced firing his cannon, crashing through obstacles, and even swimming in the English Channel with the help of large canvas airbags to keep him afloat. Despite his best efforts, Sherman wasn't as fast or as accurate as the other tanks.

"I'm not sure I'm ready for this," he said to Willy. "I give my best effort in target practice, but I always get the lowest score. Today we practiced crashing through brick walls and over fences, but I finished last. Finally, we had to swim across a river, but the other tanks had already crossed and were waiting for me before I had gone halfway."

We had to swim across a river, but the other tanks had already crossed and were waiting for me before I had gone half way.

"That's okay, Sherman, you'll become faster with practice," Willy replied.

Sherman continued as if he hadn't heard a word Willy said. "The worst thing about this is Bulldog. He constantly teases me in front of the other tanks. Yesterday, he said, 'You couldn't hit the broad side of a barn if you tried.' Today, he said, 'You swim as slow as a turtle and shouldn't even be here.'

"The other tanks look up to him as their leader and agree with him. Training seems to be so easy for him," Sherman said. "He's the best shooter, the fastest swimmer, and the strongest tank on land. I wish I could be that good."

"You will," Willy declared with confidence. "I know you'll get better. Don't let Bulldog bother you. Just focus on doing your best."

So Sherman did exactly what Willy said, and slowly, he improved.

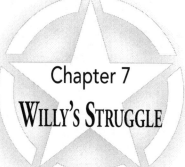

Chapter 7
WILLY'S STRUGGLE

You will never reach higher ground if you are
always pushing others down.

—Jeffrey Benjamin

Willy trained to carry soldiers and supplies to the front lines. He also practiced picking up wounded soldiers and taking them to the hospital. Willy worked hard trying to prove to the other jeeps that he was the best. However, this effort distracted him from doing his job right. He was often careless and dropped supplies, or got in the way of other jeeps as he rushed around.

He was often careless and dropped supplies or got in the way
of other jeeps as he rushed around.

One night, Sherman noticed something different
about his friend. "You're not your old self, Willy. Is
anything bothering you?"

"Yeah," Willy replied. "Yesterday, I got lost because
I didn't listen closely to orders the officer gave me.
After I was found and brought back to camp, Butch,
another jeep, blurted out, 'Hey, everyone, here comes
Wandering Willy!' Now everyone calls me Wandering
Willy. Today, he said, 'Take this ammunition to the
soldiers on the other side of that barn. Follow the
pathway through that gate and you'll find them.'

"I wanted to prove to everyone that I was the
fastest jeep around, so I charged through the gate at
full speed. Quickly, my wheels sank in deep, heavy

mud and I was hopelessly stuck in the middle of a pigpen! Everyone laughed at the sight of me covered in mud and pig poo. Then Butch smirked and said, 'So, you are going to win this war by yourself, huh?' I think Butch wants me to fail."

I was hopelessly stuck in the middle of a pigpen.

Willy looked down and said, in frustration, "It seems like the harder I try, the worse I do." He paused for a moment. Then Willy's lights flashed and, looking up, he said with a firm voice, "I'll show them. I'm going to win this war by myself. I'm not afraid of anything!"

"Willy," said Sherman, "it's not all about you. To be successful and win this war, we'll all have to work together as a team. One machine can't do everything. You must do your part and let others do their part. War is not a game, and you can get hurt if you're not careful." He added, "To be honest, I'm kinda scared. I don't know if I'm ready for this."

"Don't worry, Sherman," Willy answered. "Remember, we'll stick together, and I'll take care of you."

"I'll take care of you too, little buddy," said Sherman, sounding a bit more sure of himself.

* * *

Six months passed as preparations for the Normandy invasion and the liberation of Europe continued. A rare forecast of low ocean tides and a full moon for the night of June 4th made conditions ideal to cross the English Channel.

"Soldiers, it's time to head to the harbor this morning and board ships to cross the channel for France," the commanding officer said on June 4th. "Tomorrow is the day you've been training for. It's time for the invasion to begin. June 5th will be D-Day!"

"Oh boy!" Willy exclaimed, revving his engine. "Now is my chance to prove myself. I can't wait!"

"Slow down," Sherman said. "Let's stick together like we planned. I think we're going to need each other."

Chapter 8
CROSSING THE CHANNEL

Valor is stability, not of legs and arms, but of courage and the soul.

—Michel de Montaigne

O n the afternoon of June 4th, the seaport of Portland, England, was alive with men and equipment moving about like an army of ants. Officers barked out commands through large bullhorns so the soldiers would hear them over the tumult.

"Get those supplies on that boat!"

"All tanks, gather by that dock and prepare to board the ship!"

"Soldiers, proceed to your assigned area and wait for your order to board that landing craft!"

The reality of what lay ahead began to sink into Willy's thoughts. In an uneasy voice, he said, "Stay close to me, Sherman. If we stick together, maybe they will put us on the same boat."

Just then, an officer yelled to Sherman, "You! Go over there with the other tanks."

Willy's heart froze. He would not be with his best friend when he needed him the most.

"I'll see you on the beach, Willy," Sherman shouted as he joined the line of tanks already boarding a waiting ship.

"Be careful, Sherman," Willy shouted back. But his voice cracked. What would he do without his friend? A wave of loneliness swept over Willy. His boastful confidence from the past faded as he rolled onto the ship with the other jeeps. *Will I ever see Sherman again?*

After being loaded, the ships remained tied to the docks for hours.

"Let's get this show going! What's the holdup?" a dockworker yelled when a sailor poked his head out of the wheelhouse.

"Orders are to postpone the invasion until tomorrow. The weather report shows a storm is moving over the English Channel, and it's too rough to cross," was the reply.

There was a collective groan from the crew.

"Does that mean everything stays on the ship, or do we unload?"

"The soldiers can get off and wait on shore, but the equipment will stay aboard."

"Another day on this ship and I'll go crazy," complained the jeep next to Willy.

"Yeah," Willy replied, "I was hoping to get the waiting part of this over, but now we have to sit on this ship and think about it for another day." Butterflies in Willy's engine refused to rest as the hours of boredom passed.

Sherman fared no better. Stuck in the hold of a transport ship, the tanks were packed fender to fender on all sides. Worse yet, Bulldog was parked directly behind him. This made Sherman as nervous as the upcoming D-Day. All the tanks were quiet, even Bulldog, as they thought about their upcoming swim to shore and the battle on the beach.

Finally, Willy's and Sherman's ships sailed out of Portland Harbour the evening of June 5th, and crossed the English Channel. They were joined by thousands of other ships carrying soldiers, equipment, and supplies from other ports, all bound for the five beaches of Normandy, France.

British soldiers headed for Sword Beach and Gold Beach. Canadian soldiers sailed for Juno Beach. And the Americans headed for Utah Beach and Omaha Beach. Throughout the night, rough waves rolled the ships from side to side. Willy and the other jeeps were drenched with salt water that sprayed over the railings.

On the morning of June 6th, heavy gray clouds hid the sun and a cold wind blew across the choppy water off Omaha Beach. Planes roared overhead, dropping bombs that sent sand, smoke, and fire high into the air. The thunder of battleships' big guns pounded the air and rattled Willy's hood. Flashes of fire shot up from the beach as the defenders fired back.

"What a sight!" the jeep next to Willy exclaimed. "Have you ever seen so many ships and planes!"

Willy could only shake his head silently. He was too frightened to say a word.

What a sight! Have you ever seen so many ships and planes!

Chapter 9
THE LANDING

Hardship often prepares an ordinary person for an extraordinary destiny.

—C. S. Lewis

At 6:30 a.m., the landing ramp of Sherman's ship dropped open with a splash, framing a picture of the scene they were about to enter. Angry waves crashed against the ship's hull. Far ahead lay the beach where many obstacles were placed to prevent them from landing on shore. Explosions, fire, and smoke cast a gloomy haze over the sand and surf.

"All right, you guys," an officer called out. "Get in the water and head for the beach."

"Remember to stick together as we swim to shore," Bulldog shouted. "The faster tanks stick with me." He glanced at Sherman and added, "Slower tanks follow behind."

Sherman, along with the other tanks, rolled down the ramp, into the cold, dark water. Tanks had to swim ashore before the troops, to provide protection when their landing craft arrived.

"Follow me and I'll lead you to the beach," Bulldog shouted. "Sherman! Get out of our way. We don't want your swimming to slow us down."

The other tanks silently followed. As usual, Sherman fell behind. Artillery shells exploded around him, sending spouts of water skyward. Waves splashed in his face, and he saw many tanks begin to sink as the rough waves filled their flotation bags with water. Enemy fire hit other tanks, and they burst into flames. Sherman fixed his eyes on the beach ahead and kept swimming.

"I've got to make it to the beach for Willy," he kept repeating aloud. Halfway to shore, Sherman heard a desperate cry: "Someone help me, I'm drowning!"

Looking to his left, he spotted Bulldog, slowly sinking in the swells. Artillery shells from the enemy's heavy weapons were bursting nearer and nearer to him. None of the other tanks responded to his calls. Many of them were also sinking and the few remaining wouldn't risk their lives to help. At the end of the line of tanks, along came Sherman.

"Sherman, help me!" Bulldog shouted.

Sherman strained as he pulled Bulldog through the churning surf.

Sherman hesitated. Every bolt in his body commanded him: *Ignore this bully and get to shore. Don't risk your life for that guy.* A higher voice within him said, *In spite of what he has done or said, you need to help him, or he will drown.* Sherman had to make a decision ….

"Hold on, Bulldog. I'll be right there."

He slowly turned and swam through the hail of enemy fire … to Bulldog's side.

"Take hold of my chain," Sherman yelled, "and we'll get to shore together."

Sherman strained as he pulled Bulldog through the churning surf. Finally, they reached shallow water.

Sherman pushed Bulldog onto the beach, and said, "I'll shield you from enemy fire while you drain the water from inside you."

"Thanks, Sherman," Bulldog said. "If it weren't for you, I never would have made it."

Bulldog's superior attitude and mean spirit toward Sherman flowed out of him with the salt water. He knew Sherman had chosen to save his life despite Bulldog's mean treatment of him. Bulldog wanted to apologize for his past attitude, but that would have to wait. The battle was raging around them, and the soldiers urgently needed them for protection.

Chapter 10
BATTLE ON THE BEACH

*Courage is contagious. When a brave man takes
a stand, the spines of others are often stiffened.*

—Billy Graham

When Willy's tires rolled onto the beach, he felt the ground shake from explosions, and the loud noise of battle drowned out all other sounds. Bullets whizzed past his headlights like angry bees. The air was filled with smoke and the oily smell of burning equipment.

Now he remembered Sherman's words: "War is not a game, and you can get hurt if you're not careful."

Even though he had his own worries, Willy refused to give in to his fears. He encouraged the other jeeps that sat motionless, paralyzed with fear. "Come on, guys. This is what we've trained for. You can do it! Follow me."

Willy supplied soldiers with ammunition and carried the wounded to safety. The other jeeps soon followed his example, which helped the soldiers advance up the beach. Willy raced past many jeeps that were disabled or destroyed because of the fierce enemy fire. Suddenly, through the dust and the smoke, he spotted a jeep hopelessly tangled in barbed wire.

Willy rushed over to its side and yelled, "Take hold of my towrope!"

To Willy's surprise, a second glance at the tangled jeep revealed it was Butch.

All at once, a thunderous blast shook the ground. Dirt and rocks rained down on them like a hailstorm.

Butch shouted, "Get outta here before you're destroyed!"

Willy, acting out of instinct, threw Butch the rope. "I'm not leaving until you take hold of the rope," he yelled back.

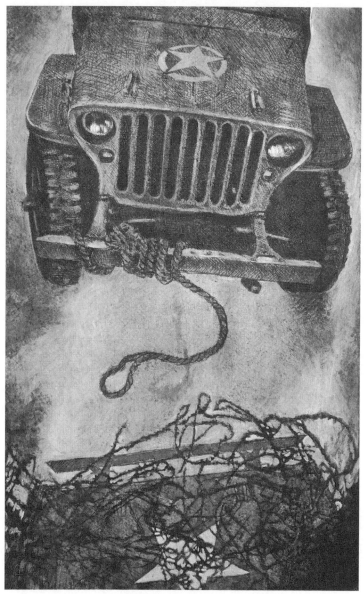

Take hold of my towrope!

Butch grabbed hold, and Willy tugged with all his strength. One by one the barbed strands broke, setting him free.

"Thanks, Willy," Butch said. "I couldn't have gotten out of there without you. I owe you one."

But Willy couldn't hear Butch because he had already disappeared into battle.

Chapter 11
SHERMAN'S CHARGE

Bravery is the capacity to perform properly even when scared half to death.

—General Omar N. Bradley

Willy's eyes constantly scanned over the uproar on the beach for his best friend. While loading supplies, he caught sight of Sherman—wet and exhausted—at the water's edge. He was one of the few tanks that had made it ashore without sinking. Willy raced across the beach to be by Sherman's side.

When Willy arrived, he heard an officer command Sherman: "I want you to lead this group of soldiers to the top of that hill and capture it. Now, move!"

Noticing the worried look on Sherman's face, Willy said, "I'll stick with you, like we agreed. We can do this together."

"Go back to your duty supplying soldiers," the officer ordered, pointing to Willy. "You'd only get in the way."

"Better do what he says," Sherman told his friend. "I'll be okay."

Sherman fired his cannon repeatedly as he crested the hilltop.

In spite of his promise to stick with Sherman, Willy had to obey. "Be careful, Sherman," Willy shouted as he turned to leave.

Sherman slowly crawled up the hill. Bullets bounced off his thick armor and mortar shells burst around him, shaking the ground and throwing stinging sand in his face. Nearly numb with fear, he kept his eyes fixed straight ahead. Sherman fired his cannon repeatedly as he crested the hilltop. The German troops defending the hill raised their hands in surrender when they saw Sherman and the American soldiers approaching.

A loud cheer erupted from the soldiers on the beach when the hilltop was captured. Now they were able to move about safely. Suddenly, a violent explosion rocked Sherman's sturdy frame. An enemy shell had hit him, and many links from both his tank tracks lay in pieces, scattered on the ground. Unable to move, he was an easy target for German fire.

Chapter 12
SAVING SHERMAN

A hero is an ordinary individual who finds the strength to persevere and endure in spite of overwhelming obstacles.

—Christopher Reeve

When Willy saw that Sherman was hit, he sprang into action. "Don't worry, Sherman," Willy cried out, "I'm coming to help!"

Grabbing some spare parts, he raced up the hill to Sherman's side.

"You need to go back down to the beach," Sherman said. "You're going to get hurt up here."

"I'm not leaving without you. Remember, we need to stick together," Willy replied.

Soldiers did their best to make temporary repairs to his tracks, and then hooked Sherman's chain to the little jeep.

Willy shifted into low gear and said to himself, *I've got to save Sherman!*

Revving his engine, he pulled with all the strength he could muster. Mud and sand flew through the air as Willy's four tires spun wildly. Slowly, he inched his friend down the hill … to a safe place away from danger.

Mud and sand flew through the air as Willy's tires spun wildly.

Now Sherman sat in an area with other wrecked tanks and jeeps. "Thanks, little buddy, you saved my life." Sherman groaned and he closed his eyes in pain. "I can't fight with you any longer. But remember, Willy, be careful, and don't try to win this war by yourself."

Willy looked sadly at Sherman as he turned again toward the battle. "I'll be back to fix you up good as new."

He returned to his duties, leaving the discouraged Sherman sitting on the beach.

Chapter 13
BRAVE WILLY

Being brave isn't the absence of fear. Being brave is having that fear but finding a way through it.

—Bear Grylls

Later that day, an officer stopped Willy and said, "Take these supplies to the soldiers on that ridge, but be careful. The fighting is fierce up there."

"Right away, sir," Willy replied, knowing that this ridge was the most dangerous area of the beach.

He bravely risked his life, speeding through the middle of combat to reach the soldiers. When he returned for more supplies, a blinding flash of light, followed by a deafening blast, toppled him onto his side. Badly damaged, dazed, and confused, he was unable to move.

When he returned for more supplies, a blinding flash of light, followed by a deafening blast, toppled him onto his side.

From where Sherman was parked, he looked up to see Willy flipped onto his side.

"I've got to save my little buddy," he said.

Regardless of his battered body and damaged tracks, he trudged inch by inch up the sandy ridge, determined to save his best friend.

Sherman finally reached Willy's side. With his chain attached, Sherman uprighted his little buddy and dragged the badly injured jeep to the bottom of the ridge.

"Thanks, Sherman," Willy moaned. "You didn't have to risk your life for me."

"Remember our promise," Sherman replied wearily. "If we stick together, you'll take care of me and I'll take care of you."

Willy and Sherman were unable to push themselves any farther.

Willy looked up at Sherman and said, "I hope this doesn't mean it's the scrapyard for us."

Sherman replied, "I don't know, but it doesn't look good."

Chapter 14
WAITING FOR THE END

No person was ever honored for what he received.
Honor has been the reward for what he gave.

—President Calvin Coolidge

Soldiers dragged Willy and Sherman to a scrapyard on the beach. It was crammed with wrecked vehicles waiting to be stripped for parts that other jeeps and tanks might need.

"I'm so sorry I couldn't have done more to save you," Willy said while oil slowly dripped from his bent frame. "Now I understand that it takes all of us to win this war, not just me."

Soldiers dragged Willy and Sherman to
a scrapyard on the beach.

Sherman gazed down at Willy's crumpled body. "You did succeed. You did your part to secure this beach so others could come ashore safely. You should be pleased with yourself."

"None of this could have been done without you capturing that hilltop," Willy replied. "You're the real hero, Sherman."

The following morning, Butch and Bulldog stopped to say good-bye to Willy and Sherman.

As it turned out, Butch rescued five soldiers on the front line who were trapped by enemy fire. For that action, he earned the reputation of being a hero. Bulldog lived up to his reputation as the best tank on the beach, by leading an advance of soldiers that captured hundreds of German troops and their artillery guns.

"We wanted to thank you guys before we advance inland with the troops," Bulldog said. "We were wrong to treat you the way we did. Please forgive us."

"Yeah," Butch added, "it's because of your selfless actions that we're still here. You two were the real heroes on the beach. We can never repay you for your sacrifice, and we'll never forget you."

Willy was a much wiser jeep now that his foolish pride was broken—along with his wrecked body.

"Remember, guys," he said, "war is not a game, and you can get hurt if you're not careful. Work as a team and we'll win."

Butch and Bulldog nodded in agreement and left, not expecting to see Willy and Sherman again.

* * *

Days passed as Willy and Sherman quietly watched new replacement jeeps and tanks safely roll over the beach they had fought so hard to win. Days turned into weeks, and weeks turned into months. During that time the Allied forces of the United States, Britain, and Canada persisted in their advance through France, toward Paris.

Soldiers continued to dismantle the wrecked vehicles for their parts. Willy's grand hope of winning the war slowly faded as he and Sherman anxiously awaited their turn to become scrap metal.

Sherman said, "No matter what happens, little buddy, we're sticking together."

Chapter 15
FAITHFUL FRIENDS

*Loyalty means nothing unless it has at its heart
the absolute principle of self-sacrifice.*

—President Woodrow Wilson

On August 25, 1944, six weeks after D-Day,
the city of Paris, France, was freed from
German control. A grand victory parade
was planned, to march through the heart of the
famous city. General Dwight Eisenhower and
General George Patton would lead the way.

When they were offered new vehicles for the
parade, both generals agreed on something.

General Eisenhower said, "How about finding a jeep and a tank that fought on Omaha Beach? We want to honor these brave machines."

An officer said, "We have the right vehicles for you."

Butch and Bulldog were selected for the position because of their brave and skillful actions on the beach.

When Butch and Bulldog heard they had been selected for this honor, Bulldog said to Butch, "We can't accept this when our friends, Willy and Sherman, are sitting in a scrapyard."

"Yeah," Butch replied, "they're the real heroes. But we must find them before it's too late."

Locating the officer in charge, Bulldog said, "This honor belongs to a brave tank that saved me from drowning the morning we swam ashore. He risked his life for me and others that day."

"And there's a jeep that saved me on the beach when it looked like I was a goner," Butch chimed in.

Bulldog said, "If they hadn't saved us, we would never have been able to do what we did."

The officer agreed. Soldiers were rushed back to the beach in search of Butch and Bulldog's friends. They had to hurry before Willy and Sherman were destroyed.

Chapter 16
THE BIG SURPRISE

I believe it is the nature of people to be heroes, given the chance.

—James A. Autry

The following morning, on the Normandy beach, soldiers from the wrecking crew collected their tools and headed to the scrapyard.

"Finally, we're down to the last jeep and tank to dismantle," a soldier said. "It'll be nice to get this area cleaned up."

As they walked toward Willy and Sherman, an officer pulled up in a jeep. "Stop! The two vehicles over there are not to be scrapped," he commanded. "The top brass wants them restored as soon as possible. I want to see them in Paris by the end of tomorrow, looking like they just rolled off the assembly line!"

Willy and Sherman watched the group of soldiers approach with wrenches and cutting torches in their hands.

"This is it, Willy. Our time is up," Sherman said softly. "There's not a better jeep in this army than you. It's been an honor serving with you."

"You're the bravest tank in the army, Sherman," Willy replied, struggling to get the words out. "I'll always remember you."

"Okay, men," barked the soldier in charge, "we've got twenty-four hours to make these two wrecks look like new. Now let's get to work!"

To their surprise, instead of being taken apart, Willy and Sherman were being rebuilt for a new life. Sparks flew, bolts turned, and fresh paint transformed them into renewed fighting machines.

"I can't believe what's happening!" Willy exclaimed. "Why are you restoring us?"

"I don't know," a mechanic answered. "We're only following orders."

Sparks flew, bolts turned, and fresh paint transformed
them into renewed fighting machines.

Willy looked at the handsome Sherman and said, "You look like a brand-new tank."

"Thanks, little buddy. And you look as good as the day you rolled off the assembly line in Toledo," answered Sherman, while a soldier finished painting a white star on his side. "I hope we can serve together wherever they send us."

"Don't worry, Sherman. With you and me fighting together, we'll win this war—"

"With the rest of the army," Sherman said firmly.

Willy smiled and said, "You're right. With the rest of the army."

Chapter 17
VICTORY PARADE

The tide has turned! The free men of the world are marching together to victory .... We will accept nothing less than full victory!

—General Dwight D. Eisenhower

Willy and Sherman were loaded onto a special train and rushed to Paris for the parade. News spread of their heroic stories. French citizens lined the tracks and waved enthusiastically as the train sped past.

"Look at all the people. Why are they waving?" Willy asked with a puzzled expression.

"It looks like they're waving at us, but it must be at someone important," Sherman answered.

At the station, Willy and Sherman were lifted off the train. Camera bulbs flashed and news reporters crowded around them to hear the commander tell of their brave actions.

"I must be dreaming this," Willy said. "How did everyone find out about what we did?"

"I have no idea," Sherman answered.

"All right. Get these vehicles to the parade, now!" the commander ordered the soldiers.

Willy asked, "What parade is this?"

"Oh, you'll find out soon enough," the commander said.

Before long, they arrived at the parade grounds and were positioned in front of hundreds of jeeps, tanks, and soldiers waiting to begin. Butch and Bulldog were standing directly behind them, wearing big smiles.

"Nice to see you could make it here," Bulldog said.

"We saved that place for you guys," Butch added.

Willy and Sherman were wide-eyed and speechless at what was happening.

Within a few minutes, to their even greater surprise, General Eisenhower and General Patton strode up to them and saluted. Willy's horn beeped and his engine revved with excitement when General Eisenhower climbed in and sat on his front seat. Then General Patton climbed up Sherman and took his place on top.

"Welcome aboard,'" Sherman said sheepishly.

General Patton smiled and nodded.

Sherman felt a pride in himself that he had never experienced before. He glanced down as Willy impatiently crept forward.

"Willy, behave yourself," Sherman whispered sternly.

At General Eisenhower's command, the long lines of jeeps and tanks started their engines. "Let's give these heroes the honor they deserve," he announced.

The parade of military vehicles began to roll slowly down the main avenue, with Willy and Sherman proudly leading the way.

Men and women lined the streets, cheering loudly and waving flags. Children ran alongside and showered all the vehicles with flowers. Although the war was far from over, the parade offered everyone a brief escape from the thoughts of war, and an opportunity to celebrate Paris' freedom from German rule.

The parade of military vehicles began to roll slowly down the main avenue, with Willy and Sherman proudly leading the way.

That evening, after the parade had finished, Willy, Sherman, Butch, and Bulldog ended the day in a holding yard for jeeps and tanks. The newly formed friends recalled the day's events until the early hours of the morning.

"I still can't believe what happened today," Willy said. "Leading the parade, watching everyone cheer us, and carrying General Eisenhower—it's like a dream. Remember the day we joked about carrying the generals in a victory parade? I never imagined that would actually happen."

"If ever there are two vehicles that deserve this honor, it's both of you," Bulldog said as Butch nodded in agreement.

Sherman looked at Willy. "Remember the promise we made to be there for each other? That's what got us through all the hard times, and that's the reason we're here tonight. We did it together. I'm lucky to have such a good friend as you."

Willy blinked his lights and replied, "And I'm so thankful for a loyal friend like you, Sherman."

* * *

It would be almost a year before total victory in Europe would be accomplished, and they were uncertain of what lay ahead. But for the moment, they enjoyed their new friendships together and a well-deserved rest.

P.S. More than seventy years later, Willy and Sherman remain best friends.

Willy and Sherman remain best friends.

THE END

I hope you've enjoyed reading *Willy and Sherman: Battle on the Beach*.

Look for the sequel, *Willy and Sherman: Battle of the Bulge*, where Willy and Butch are surrounded by the enemy in the small town of Bastogne, in Belgium. Sherman and Bulldog, along with General Patton's army, are called on to save them. However, without the help of a twelve-year-old girl, that will be impossible.

Interesting Facts

1. The jeep was the first American four-wheel-drive vehicle. More than 643,000 jeeps were produced for the war.

2. No one knows for sure where the name "jeep" came from. One possible answer was from the cartoon character, Popeye the Sailor, and his magical pet, Eugene the jeep, who could go anywhere.

3. Stars were placed on United States military vehicles. A star surrounded by a circle was painted on the hood or roof of vehicles used on D-Day. This symbol identified them as allied vehicles to the attacking planes flying over head. It was called an invasion star.

4. Soldiers loved the jeep. General Eisenhower said the jeep was a big reason the Allies won the war.

5. General Dwight D. Eisenhower was America's top general in Europe. He later became the 34th president of the United States.

6. The Sherman tank was named after General Sherman of the Union Army in the Civil War.

7. A Sherman tank weighed as much as twenty-seven jeeps put together. It was America's most widely-used tank of the war.

8. General George Patton was a great American tank commander in World War 2. He was very demanding of his soldiers.

9. Many convoys (large groups of supply ships) crossed the Atlantic Ocean to England. German submarines often attacked convoys.

10. The Germans had built defenses called the Atlantic Wall, along the French coast. It contained many protected guard posts (pillboxes) and big guns.

11. Operation Overlord was the code name for the invasion of Normandy, France. It came to be known as D-Day.

12. D-Day is a military term for Invasion Day.

13. Until the very last minute, Operation Overlord was kept top secret so the Germans wouldn't find out where it would take place.

14. The planners of D-Day needed a very rare combination of low tide, a moonlit night, and good weather to carry out the invasion.

15. The invasion site was fifty miles long and divided into five landing beaches. Juno, Gold, and Sword beaches were invaded by the Canadians and the British. The United States invaded Utah and Omaha beaches.

16. D-Day was an important step in liberating Europe from German control.

17. As many as 6,939 naval vessels transported 156,000 soldiers across the English Channel to Normandy, France, on D-Day.

18. Because of rough waves, twenty-seven out of thirty-two tanks sank as they approached Omaha Beach.

19. Many soldiers drowned trying to get to shore because they carried so much heavy gear.

20. The soldiers were given little clickers to identify other American soldiers at night. If you heard a "click," you knew the soldier was American.

21. The Normandy invasion was the largest military operation in history.

For additional interesting facts and links to resources, visit www.DaveDeVisser.com.

D-DAY INVASION MAP

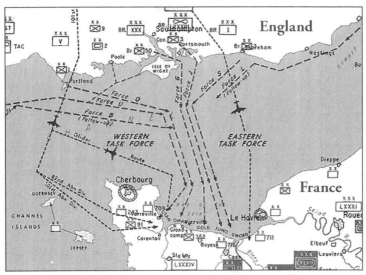

WWII was the largest armed conflict in world history, extending around the entire globe and involving more countries than any war before it. This war was fought to stop the takeover of Europe by: Adolf Hitler, from Germany; Benito Mussolini, of Italy; and countries of the Far East, led by Emperor Michinomiya Hirohito, of Japan.

Millions of men, women, and children perished during the war years of 1939 to 1945. Many accounts of bravery and heroism by soldiers and civilians were also recorded.

The invasion of Normandy, France, on D-Day, marked a turn in Europe's war—in favor of the Allies.

WORLD WAR 2 PHOTOGRAPHS

General Eisenhower speaking to the soldiers before D-Day
(United States National Archives)

Jeep being loaded onto an airplane glider.
(ww2dbase United States Army)

American troops watch activity on the beach at Normandy beach.
(United States National Archives)

Troops leave their landing craft and wade to shore at
Normandy beach. (United States National Archives)

A jeep being lowered into a landing craft headed for the beach.
(ww2dbase United States Navy)

Sherman tank leaving an LST (landing ship tank).
(United States National Archives)

Sherman tank with airbags at Normandy beach.
(ww2dbase United States Marine Corps Robert Bare Collection)

Sherman tank towing a disabled truck on Normandy beach.
(Imperial War Museum)

Sherman tank with a waterproof float bag.
(Imperial War Museum)

Sherman tank lifting a section of a bridge.
(United States Army Signal Corps)

Sherman tank in action.
(ww2dbase Imperial War Museum)

Bantam jeep goes airborne.
(ww2dbase Library of Congress)

Jeep on the USS *Yorktown* being used to pull airplanes.
(ww2dbase United States Navy)

Jeep in front of the Eiffel Tower after liberating France.
(ww2dbase Library of Congress)

Assembly plant for Sherman tanks near Detroit, Michigan.
(ww2dbase Detroit Public Library)

For additional interesting photographs and links to resources, visit www.DaveDeVisser.com.

Acknowledgments

I never considered writing a book until, at the age of sixty, a story began to stir within me. Without formal training or experience in writing, I sought help from others.

My wife Joan has been a tremendous help from the beginning. She assisted with shaping this story and encouraged me from day one. Without her work, this book would not exist.

Joy Witte, a good friend and my fifth-grade teacher, helped with editing in the early stages of the story. Her encouragement and belief that I could write have meant a lot to me.

Thanks go to my family and friends who read the first drafts of the book and gave me valuable input. A special thanks to my daughter Allison Struber for her research and enthusiasm.

Others who played a big part in this book are: Cary VanderVeen for his excellent illustrations, Leslie Helakoski for content editing, Beth Mansbridge for copyediting, and Frances Keiser for the design and layout of the book. I also want to thank David Stubblebine and World War 2 Database for help with the photographs.

ABOUT THE AUTHOR

Dave DeVisser's interest in World War II history began fifteen years ago when he purchased and restored a 1942 military jeep with his friend Dave Scheffers. Since then, he has built an extensive library of books on the history of the war. Dave is a member of the Military Vehicle Preservation Association (MVPA) and the Society of Children's Book Writers and Illustrators (SCBWI).

Dave enjoys displaying his jeep and sharing his knowledge at veterans' Honor Flight Tours and other events. Dave's father was a veteran of WW2, serving in the Philippine Islands and Okinawa.

The motivation to write this story originated in Dave's desire to spark children's interest in the history of WW2 and show them the value of loyal friendships.

About the Illustrator

Cary VanderVeen has been an artist most of his life. When Cary was a young boy, his father gave him a crow quill pen and taught him how to draw with pen and ink. When Cary was thirteen, his grandmother gave him her watercolor brushes. He still uses the pen and the brushes.

Cary has a bachelor's degree in fine art and art education, and a master's degree in painting. He has taught art for more than thirty years in public and private schools. Over the years, Cary has been in art organizations, art shows and art competitions, and his artwork is a part of many private collections.

Made in the USA
Middletown, DE
19 November 2018